First published in Great Britain by Pelham Books Ltd
44 Bedford Square   London WC1B 3DP   1985

This edition first published in Denmark by Gyldendal Boghandel 1985

Illustrations Copyright © Svend Otto S. 1985

English translation Copyright © Pelham Books Ltd 1985

All Rights Reserved. No part of this publication may be
reproduced, stored in a retrieval system, or transmitted
in any form or by any means, electronic, mechanical,
photocopying, recording or otherwise, without the prior
permission of the Copyright owner.

ISBN 0 7207 1625 x

Phototypeset in Great Britain by Tradespools Ltd, Frome, Somerset
Printed in Portugal.

Aesop

THE FOX AND THE STORK

Illustrated by

Svend Otto S.

Twenty fables re-told by Joan Tate

PELHAM BOOKS

The Lion and the Mouse

A lion was once sleeping in the grass and a mouse came along and woke it. It had not meant to, but the lion was angry and grabbed the mouse with its great paw.

"I'm going to eat you," cried the lion.

"Oh, please don't," said the mouse. "I'm so small. There are lots of big animals. They're much tastier. Please let me go, and one day I'll do something for you in exchange."

The lion smiled.

"I can't imagine what a little creature like you could do for me, the King of the Beasts," said the lion. And it let the mouse go.

A few days later, the mouse heard a terrible roaring. It was the lion, caught in a net some huntsmen had put out.

The lion was struggling in the net, but the ropes were too strong and it could not break them. The mouse could see this and at once started nibbling at the ropes. It wasn't long before it had gnawed right through.

That was how the weak little mouse saved the big strong lion.

The Wolf and the Lamb

A thirsty wolf once went down to a stream to drink. There was a lamb there, a little further down the stream. The lamb was drinking, too.

"How dare you muddy the water I am to drink," growled the wolf.

"How can I muddy your water," said the lamb. "It runs from you to me, not the other way round."

"That may be," said the wolf. "But you were very rude to me a year ago."

"Me?" said the lamb. "I wasn't even born a year ago."

"Well, if it wasn't you, then it was your father," roared the wolf. "I won't stand for such insolence!"

And the wolf leapt on the lamb and gobbled it up.

The Kid and the Wolf

A kid once strayed from the flock and was followed by a wolf. The kid tried to save its life by running away, but it was no good.

When the kid saw that there was no hope of escape, it turned and faced the wolf.

"I know you will eat me," said the kid. "But if my life is to be short, I'd like it to be a merry one. Please play your flute."

The wolf liked the idea of some music before his dinner, and started playing.

But some dogs heard the music and ran up to see what was going on. The wolf turned and ran away as fast as its legs would carry it.

The Old Man and Death

An old woodman gathered up a huge bundle of sticks. He heaved it on to his back and started walking back to his hut. On the way, he grew so tired, he let the bundle of sticks fall to the ground and sat down beside it.

"Oh, wretched creature that I am," he sighed. "If only Death would come and deliver me from all this misery."

Death arrived at that very moment and said to the old man: "You called for me. Here I am. What do you want of me?"

The old man was very frightened.

"Please would you help me get my bundle of sticks up on to my back again," he said. "So that I can go on."

The Dog and its Reflection

A dog had stolen a piece of meat and run away with it. On its way, it came to a small bridge. Then it saw its reflection in the water.

"Look at that," said the dog to itself. "There's another dog. It's got a piece of meat, too. And what's more, its piece is bigger than mine. I want that piece."

The dog let its own piece of meat go and grabbed at the other dog's. But at that very moment, the other dog and its meat vanished and the dog's piece of meat floated away downstream.

So the greedy dog made a fool of itself.

The Thirsty Crow

A crow was once very thirsty. Then it found a pitcher. Right at the bottom of the pitcher was a little water. But the crow couldn't reach it.

The crow tried tipping the pitcher over, but it was much too heavy and the crow was much too weak.

What should it do? The crow thought and thought, and at last had an idea.

The crow picked up a little stone and dropped it into the pitcher. Then it picked up another, and yet another.

The water in the pitcher began to rise. When the crow saw this, it collected up more and more stones and dropped them into the pitcher.

In the end, the water rose right to the top and the clever crow could reach it and drink as much as it wanted.

The Wolf and the Crane

A wolf once had a bone stuck in its throat and was about to choke to death. It promised gold and all kinds of treasures to anyone who would come and help get the bone out. But no one was brave enough.

Then a crane came along.

"Please save my poor life, brother crane," begged the wolf. "I'll reward you well for your services."

"That's a good promise," said the crane.

It thrust its long beak down the wolf's throat and pulled out the bone.

Then the crane asked for the reward.

"How dare you ask for a reward," growled the wolf. "Think yourself lucky I didn't bite your head off when it was in my mouth."

The Shepherd Boy and the Wolf

A shepherd boy was guarding a flock of sheep outside a village.

Just for fun he shouted: "The wolf's coming! The wolf's coming! Wolf! Wolf!"

The villagers hurried out to chase the wolf away. But there was no wolf. They saw that the shepherd boy was joking. They went back home and the boy laughed to himself for having fooled them.

He tried the same joke again. Three times, he fooled the villagers.

But one fine day, the wolf really did come. The boy cried out as before: "The wolf's coming! The wolf's coming! Wolf! Wolf!"

But the villagers thought the boy was joking again. So they took no notice of his shouts and the wolf killed every single one of the sheep.

The Donkey in the Lion's Skin

A donkey once found a lion's skin and put it on. Then it went round frightening all the other animals.

The donkey saw a fox and said to itself: "I'll give that little fox a real fright."

But the fox heard the donkey.

"I would certainly have been very frightened," the fox said. "If you'd had the sense to keep your mouth shut."

The Fox and the Raven

A raven stole a piece of cheese and flew up into a tree with it. The fox saw this and ran under the tree.

"Oh, raven!" said the fox. "How handsome you are! No bird in the world has such lovely glossy feathers as you have. If only your voice matched your black costume, you would be the most beautiful of birds!"

The raven was pleased to hear the fox's praises. It liked the fine words and wished to show that it also had a fine voice. So it began to caw, but as soon as it opened its beak, it dropped the cheese.

The cheese fell straight down to the fox, who snapped up the delicious morsel.

The Two Friends and the Bear

Two friends were out together in the forest, when a bear came along. One man quickly climbed up a tree and hid. The other man could do nothing against such a large animal on his own, and it was too late to escape. But he had heard that bears never touch dead people. So he lay down on the ground and pretended to be dead.

The bear went up and sniffed at him. But the man held his breath and didn't move. The bear left him there and lolloped on.

When it had gone, the other man came down from the tree.

"What did the bear say to you?" he asked. "I saw it whispering something in your ear."

"It gave me some good advice," said the other man.

"What was that?" said the first man.

"It told me not to walk with friends who leave you in the lurch."

Father, Son and Donkey

A man and his son bought a donkey and took it home with them. Both of them were very pleased. On the way, they met a horseman. "You are stupid!" he cried. "Surely your donkey is not so small it can't carry one of you?"

"The man's right," said the son. "Up you get, Father." The father climbed on to the donkey and on they went.

Then a woman came along. "That's not very nice of you," she said. "Riding along and letting that poor boy walk alongside you." So the father got down and the son climbed on to the donkey.

Then two old men came along. "Look at that idle boy!" they said. "Letting his poor old father do the walking."

So both the father and son climbed on to the donkey and on they rode. Then a young girl came along. "What a disgrace!" she said. "That poor creature having to carry two big strong men. If there was any justice in the world, it would be the other way round, and you should be carrying the poor beast."

So what did the two of them do?

They tied the donkey's legs together, put a pole between them and tried to carry the animal home.

No one knows how far they got.

The Hare and the Tortoise

A hare was jeering at a tortoise because it was so slow.

"Shall we have a race?" said the tortoise. "Although my legs are short, I'll probably beat you."

"I'd like to see that!" laughed the hare. "Let's try."

The tortoise took the race very seriously and trundled off. But the hare thought it all a great joke and amused itself rolling about and turning somersaults in the grass. It was relying on its quick legs.

"I've plenty of time to take a little nap," thought the hare. "I'll get there long before that old plodder."

So the hare lay down and went to sleep.

Meanwhile, the tortoise was trundling along, going very very slowly, but it kept walking on.

At last the hare woke up and was suddenly very busy. It rushed off like a whirlwind, but when it got to the goal, the tortoise was already there.

The Fox and the Stork

One day, the fox invited the stork to dinner. They were to have soup and the fox served it on a shallow plate.

The stork did its best to eat with its long narrow beak, but was unable to get as much as a single drop. So it just stayed hungry and watched the fox eating up all the food.

"I hope you've had enough," said the fox.

"Yes, thank you, a delicious meal," said the stork. "I hope in return you will come and have dinner with me tomorrow?"

The fox arrived and when it was time for dinner, the stork gave him a delicious-smelling stew. But it had put the food into a long-necked jar and the fox couldn't get its nose into it. It had to be content with just licking round the top.

The fox did not get very fat on that, and the stork ate up all the food itself. When the jar was empty, the stork burped loudly.

"I hope you've had enough," said the stork to the fox. "And thank you for yesterday's dinner."

The Council of Mice

The mice once held a meeting. They talked about how they could possibly get rid of their great enemy, the cat. They listened to many plans and arguments and suggestions. But nothing was decided.

At last a young mouse stepped forward. "I have a plan," said the young mouse. "We know the cat catches us because we never hear it coming. So let's tie a bell round its neck. Then we'll hear it coming and we can escape."

This was greeted with great applause and was agreed on. But then an old mouse stepped forward. "I am in full agreement with the honoured speaker," said the old mouse. "The suggestion is a good one. But tell me, just who is going to tie the bell on?"

"That's easy," said the young mouse. "We'll form a committee."

That's what they did, and they're still sitting there talking about it.

The Mouse and the Frog

A mouse once wanted to get across a river, but it couldn't swim. So it asked a frog to help it.

"Tie your foot to my foot," the frog said. "Then I'll swim across and pull you along with me."

The mouse did as it was told. But when they were out on the water, the frog dived down and tried to drown the mouse. The poor creature struggled to get free. A hungry eagle saw them and swooped down and caught the mouse. But it took the frog with it and gobbled up them both.

The Fox and the Woodman

A fox was once fleeing from some huntsmen. It ran and ran, looking for somewhere to hide. It came to a woodman and asked him to help. The woodman did. He hid the fox under a heap of branches.

Shortly afterwards, along came the huntsmen. "Hullo, woodman," they said. "Have you seen a fox anywhere around here?"

"No, I've seen no foxes," said the woodman. But as he said it, he pointed at the place where the fox was hiding. But the huntsmen didn't understand.

When they had gone, the fox came out and went away without saying thank-you.

The woodman shouted after the fox. "Ungrateful beast!" he cried. "Why didn't you thank me? I saved your life."

"I would have liked to thank you and pay you," said the fox. "If I hadn't seen your finger saying yes and your mouth saying no."

The Mouse and the Snail

A mouse once met a snail meandering along with its house on its back.

"I'm very glad I don't have to drag my house along with me wherever I go," squeaked the mouse. "You'll wear yourself out. It takes you a whole day to go as far as I go in ten minutes."

"You're quite right, mouse dear," said the snail. "You're very quick afoot. But it's a pity your enemy the cat can run even faster than you can. You often have to race from place to place to find somewhere to hide. Then you'd probably like to change places with me and my heavy load."

The Fox that Ate Too Much

One day, a fox was out in the forest looking for food. It was very thin and very hungry. It saw a hollow oak tree, and inside the trunk was a sack full of sausages, meat, cheese and bread. A thief had hidden them there.

The fox squeezed its way through the opening in the hollow tree and gobbled everything up, so that it became as fat as a football.

But when the fox wanted to get out again, it got stuck in the opening and could get neither in nor out.

The fox sighed and groaned and was very miserable.

Another fox came along and asked what was the matter.

The fox explained and the other fox said: "You are in a fix, my friend."

"Yes, I realise that," said the first fox. "But how shall I get out of it?"

"As far as I can see," said the second fox. "There's only one thing you can do. You must stay where you are and wait until you're as thin as you were before. Then you'll easily get out. You see, I've read that time heals all wounds."

The Art of Reading

One day, a fox saw a horse. It had never seen one before, so was frightened and ran away. Then the fox met a wolf. "I've seen a very strange creature," the fox said to the wolf. "It's like a large donkey. But I'm frightened, because I don't know what it's called."

"Let's go and find out," said the wolf.

So together they went to the horse.

"What are you called?" the wolf asked.

"I've forgotten," said the horse. "But my name's written on my right hind hoof. You can see it there if you know the art of reading."

"Well, I've never been to school," said the fox. "But I'd still very much like to know your name."

"I can do it," said the wolf. "I can read words and writing."

The horse raised its hind leg so that the wolf could see the nails in the horse-shoe. They did indeed look like writing.

"I can see the writing," said the wolf. "But I can't make out what it says."

"Come closer, then you'll be able to," said the horse.

The wolf did so and went right up to the horse's hind leg. The horse gave the wolf such a kick that it fell down dead.

But the fox hurried away, thinking: "Reading words is not the same as understanding writing."